Sam Bennett's New Shoes

by Jennifer Thermes

Carolrhoda Books, Inc. / Minneapolis

Spring was a promise away on the day the
cobbler traveled over the hill to the Bennetts' farm.
It was a special day...

for Sam, the oldest child, was getting new shoes. Shoes were
costly, but Sam's were worn and full of holes. The new shoes
were big.

"To give you room to grow," said Papa.

"New shoes! I have new shoes!"
shouted Sam, to anyone who would listen.
The shoes were big and sturdy and
made of leather. Sam loved them.

That evening, Papa said they would hide Sam's old shoes in the wall near the chimney.

"Why, Papa?" asked Sam.

"Across the sea where I was born, my papa hid my shoes to keep us safe and fill our home with good fortune."

Sam was still puzzled.

"Like a child, shoes are filled with hope and promise," explained Papa.

Sam was filled with excitement.

That spring, Sam planted seeds while Papa plowed. He liked the way his new shoes fit in Papa's footprints in the soil.

"My new shoes make me big!" said Sam.

Sam tossed corncobs to the pigs and ran away as they bustled toward their supper.

"My new shoes make me fast!" said Sam.

Sam carried water from the well for Mama's wash and didn't spill a drop on his shoes.

"Your new shoes make you careful," said Mama.

When summer came, Sam's shoes were still too big, but Papa
said he could help with the sheep just the same.

"I'm old enough to shear the sheep!" shouted Sam, to anyone
who would listen.

Papa clipped the thick wool coats, while
Sam whispered in the sheep's velvet ears.
"Mama will spin your wool into yarn
for our clothes," he told the sheep.
Papa was pleased with Sam's help.

In autumn, Sam could still wiggle his toes in his shoes. And by the time snow fell, his feet didn't slip and slide anymore. Sam carried the wood Papa split to keep their home warm. His feet stayed cozy and dry. Snowflakes tasted cold on Sam's tongue.

During winter, the Bennetts stayed close to the hearth. Sam oiled his shoes and dried them near the fire. The wind howled outside.

"Come spring, you might be big enough to go to town with me," Papa said to Sam.

"I've never been to town before!" said Sam.

Town was many miles from home, and Papa always stayed there overnight.

I hope I'll be big enough, thought Sam.

After a long winter, spring came at last. It was time for Papa's
trip to town. Sam's shoes fit perfectly now.
    "May I go too?" asked Sam.
    "Yes," said Papa, "I'll surely need your help."

    "To town! I'm big enough to go to town!" shouted Sam,
to anyone who would listen.
    They hitched the horse to the wagon and set off over
the hill. Papa let Sam hold the reins.

Town was full of people, more than Sam had ever seen in
one place. Sam thought of Mama and his brothers back home.
He felt all grown-up walking with Papa.

The general store had barrels of goods. There were bolts of fabric from other lands and licorice sticks and spinning tops and a fruit that Sam had never seen, called an orange. Papa bought a sack of flour and one of tea. He bought a piece of loaf sugar, wrapped in paper, and a packet of marigold seeds for Mama. There were even some shiny glass marbles for Sam's brothers.

Soon the day turned even finer. In the market, Papa traded
some of Mama's homespun cloth for a pup named Molly.
She wiggled with excitement.
   "She'll make a good farm dog," said Papa.
Sam couldn't wait to take her home.

That night, Sam and Papa camped under the stars. Sam was tired, but his eyes were wide open and full of all he had seen.

"This was as good a day as when I got my new shoes," he told Molly.

In the morning, a spring rain fell as the wagon
creaked toward home.
Suddenly, they stopped. The wagon was stuck.
"Spring rain makes fine mud," said Papa.

The horse pulled on her harness. The wheels didn't move.
Papa strained against the wagon. It wouldn't budge. Even
taking out the barrel of salt cod didn't work.

Then Papa said, "Sam, I need your help."

Papa tied the reins to the seat of the wagon. Together, Sam and Papa pushed. Sam leaned with all his strength. He dug his feet into the ground. Mud seeped into his shoes.

Sam slipped. His shoes were wet and dirty. He got up.

"I can still help, Papa," said Sam, as he began to push again.

All at once, the mud sputtered, and the wheels moved. The wagon was free!

"You surely fill your shoes now,
Sam," said Papa.

Sam's left shoe was scraped.
His right one had split a seam.
But shoes could be fixed. Sam
and Papa would soon be home.

By the end of summer, Sam's shoes were tight. He tried to squeeze his toes together, but the shoes had stretched as far as they could.

"Sam, you are doing the work of a young man now," said Papa. "You should have boots."

Papa bartered two ax handles and a pair of woolen socks with the cobbler.
They were old boots, cleaned and re-stitched, but they were new to Sam.

"My first boots!" said Sam, standing tall.
Sam gave his old shoes to Caleb, his next younger brother.
"New shoes! I have new shoes!" shouted Caleb, to anyone who would listen.

In time, Caleb outgrew Sam's old shoes. He passed them down to Jonathan,

who passed them on to Matthew,

who passed them onto Isaac.

Many patches and repairs
later, the shoes were completely
worn out. They were put
upstairs, forgotten in the attic.

The years went by, and Sam grew into a fine young man. His
brothers had moved away, but Sam stayed and lived in Mama and
Papa's house with his new bride. They farmed the land together.
Soon they had a child.

"My daughter!" said Sam, too excited to say much else.

They named her Emma, and Sam built a room onto the house
in celebration. His neighbors came to help.

When the room was almost finished, Sam remembered Papa's
tradition from across the sea.

He found his favorite old shoes in the attic and hid them
in the wall of the new room.

"My papa did the same when I was a boy," whispered
Sam to his baby girl. "In time, we'll hide your shoes too."

Emma kicked her tiny feet and opened her eyes. Sam
smiled, for they were wide and filled with hope and promise.

Author's Note

Little is known about the tradition of hiding shoes, called concealments, in the walls of old houses. It was a custom brought to America by early settlers, mostly from England. Often only a single child's shoe was hidden. However, groups of shoes have also been found. Shoes have been discovered in houses dating back to the 1600s.

Historians think that people may have hidden shoes for protection and good fortune. Many people of the 1600s and 1700s believed that spirits came into houses. What could stop these spirits? A shoe molded to the shape of its owner's foot. If the shoe was hidden near a place easy for spirits to enter, such as a chimney or window, the spirit might think it found the shoe's owner and leave the rest of the house alone.

During renovations of my own home, built around the year 1720, my husband found a boot in the ceiling of a room in the house. Two years later, we found a shoe under the floorboards. It still had pieces of the wooden pegs that held it together.

Finding these treasures makes me think about the children who have lived in our home. Nobody knows for certain why children's shoes were concealed. But I imagine—what better than a child to symbolize hope and promise for the future?

For Stephen,
who found the boot and the shoe,
and for Jean
and my writing workshop friends,
with love and gratitude
—J.T.

Carolrhoda Books, Inc.
A division of Lerner Publishing Group
241 First Avenue North
Minneapolis, MN 55401 U.S.A.

Website address: www.lernerbooks.com

Library of Congress Cataloging-in-Publication Data

Thermes, Jennifer.
    Sam Bennett's new shoes / by Jennifer Thermes.
        p.   cm.
    Summary: Sam is excited about getting new shoes, and as he grows into
the shoes he becomes old enough to help his father on the farm, eventually
becoming a farmer himself.
    ISBN-13: 978−1−57505−822−1 (lib. bdg. : alk. paper)
    ISBN-10: 1−57505−822−7 (lib. bdg. : alk. paper)
    [1. Growth—Fiction. 2. Shoes—Fiction. 3. Farm life—Fiction.
4. Family life—Fiction.] I. Title.
PZ7.T35238Sam 2006
[E]—dc22   2005015000

Manufactured in the United States of America
1 2 3 4 5 6 — JR — 11 10 09 08 07 06